Level 1
Early Beginner

RIO

A TWENTIETH CENTURY FOX FILM
FROM THE CREATORS OF ICE AGE™

Blu and Jewel

Popcorn ELT Readers

Meet ... everyone from Rio

Hi! I'm **Blu**.
I am a blue Spix's Macaw. There are not many Spix's Macaws. I live in the USA.

This is **Jewel**. She is a beautiful blue Spix's Macaw. She lives in Rio in Brazil.

This is **Tulio**. He helps birds from the rainforest. Tulio loves Spix's Macaws.

Rafael

This is **Rafael**. He lives in the rainforest.

rainforest ....o

Marcel

Nigel

This is **Marcel** and his friend, **Nigel**. They are not nice.

Luiz

Luiz is a good friend of Rafael.

Rio is in Brazil. Rio is next to the rainforest. In Rio in February or March, it is **Carnival**.

Before you read ...

What do you think? Blu goes to Rio. Why?

New Words

What do these new words mean? Ask your teacher or use your dictionary.

cage

beautiful

The girl is **beautiful**.

chain

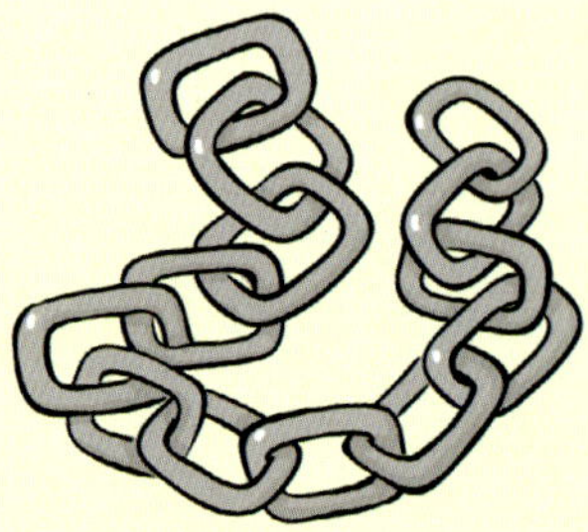

This is a **chain**.

bite

This dog **bites**!

fall

The cat is **falling**.

fly

They can **fly**.

hurt

The cat is **hurting** the boy.

free

I'm **free**!

plane

The **plane** is flying.

help

The boy is **helping** his mother.

'No problem!'

Rio
Blu and Jewel

CHAPTER ONE
'This is Rio!'

Wow! This is Rio in Brazil. It is beautiful. But it is far from my home.

Tulio lives in Rio.

'Come here, Blu,' says Tulio. 'This is your new girlfriend, Jewel.'

Jewel is beautiful.

'Hi,' I say, 'I'm Blu.'

But Jewel is angry. 'I'm not your girlfriend,' she says.

'Why are you here?' asks Jewel. 'You're not from Rio.'

Jewel doesn't like me. I'm sad and I want to go home.

That night the door opens.

'Can I go home now?' I shout.

But someone puts me in a small cage with Jewel.

'Where are we going?' asks Jewel.

Suddenly a man and a white bird look into the cage.

'Look, Nigel,' says the man. 'Not one, but TWO blue Spix's Macaws!'

'That's good, Marcel!' laughs Nigel.

Suddenly Jewel flies out of the cage and bites Marcel.

'Ow!' shouts Marcel. Then he puts a chain on me and Jewel.

'Horrible birds!' he says.

CHAPTER TWO
'I want to be free!'

Jewel bites the cage.

'What are you doing?' I ask.

'I want to be free!' she shouts.

'No problem!' I say. 'I have a cage at home. I can do it!'

I open the cage door.

'We're free!' shouts Jewel and flies out of the room with me behind her.

'No!' I shout. 'I can't fly!'

'Oh no!' says Jewel and then we fall ... CRASH! Where are we now?

We are in the rainforest. It is beautiful, but we are not happy.

'Hi,' says a bird. 'I'm Rafael. Are you coming to Carnival?'

Then Rafael sees the chain.

'My friend Luiz can help you,' he says. 'We can go to Carnival and see Luiz too!'

At Carnival, everyone is happy. Jewel and I dance, and then Jewel sings.

'She likes you!' laughs Rafael.

Suddenly we see a big dog.
'Help!' shouts Jewel.

'It's OK!' says Rafael. 'This is Luiz.'
'Can you help with the chain?' I ask.
'No problem!' says Luiz.
'Thank you, Luiz!' shouts Jewel.
Now Jewel can fly again.

CHAPTER THREE
A new home

'I'm free!' shouts Jewel.

I want to fly with Jewel, but I can't. I walk away slowly.

'Blu!' says Jewel. 'Where are you going?'

'I'm going home,' I say.

Jewel looks at me. She is sad.

I want to say 'You're beautiful', but I don't.

'I want to go home,' I say. 'I don't like it here.'

Jewel flies away.

Soon Luiz and I are at Carnival. But where is Jewel?

Then I see her. She is in a cage.

'Go away, Blu!' says Jewel.

I don't understand. But then I see Nigel.

'I've got you now!' he says.

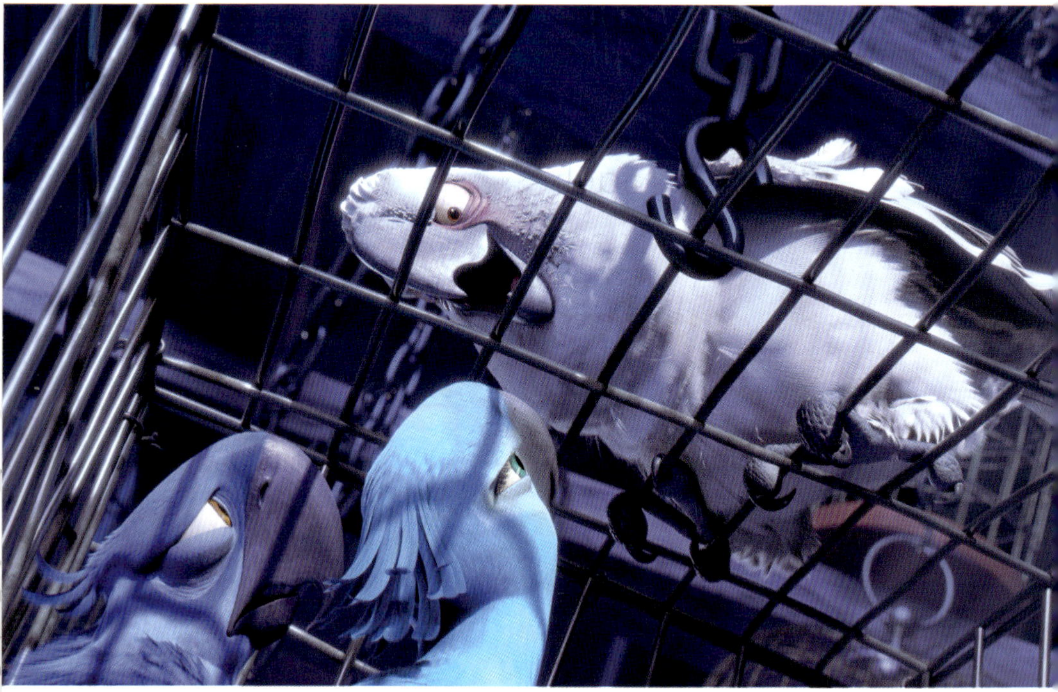

Marcel and Nigel put the cage on a plane.
'Let's fly!' shouts Marcel.

'Can you open the cage?' asks Jewel.
'No problem,' I say.
'Stop!' shouts Nigel.
I quickly open the cage.

'Quick, Jewel, go!' I shout.

Then Nigel hurts her.

'Blu! Help!' says Jewel. 'I can't fly now.' She falls out of the plane door.

I fall after her. 'I'm here, Jewel!' I say.

'Look!' she laughs. 'You're flying!'

Wow! This is Rio in Brazil. It is beautiful. And now it is my home!

THE END

Real World

Parrots

Blu and Jewel are Spix's Macaws. Macaws are a type of parrot. What do you know about parrots?

Parrot facts

- There are about 330 types of parrot.
- Some parrots live for 50 years ... or more!
- Some parrots can speak.

Parrots in danger

Many parrots live in the rainforest, but their rainforest homes are in danger. People also catch parrots because they are beautiful. About 30% of parrots are in danger.

The Spix's Macaw

The Spix's Macaw is a small parrot. It is from the rainforest in Brazil. There are no more Spix's Macaws in the rainforest. You can see them in São Paulo Zoo in Brazil.

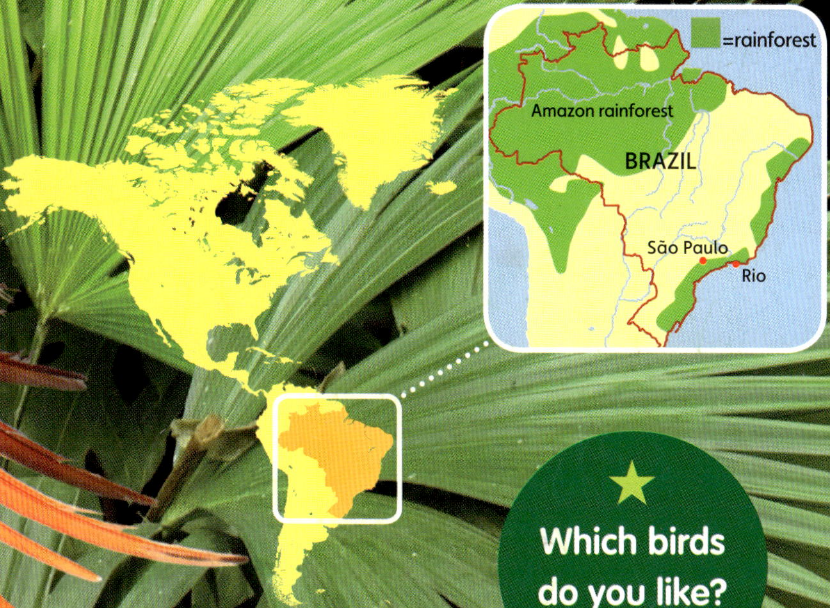

★ Which birds do you like? ★

What do these words mean? Find out.

type about in danger people catch

After you read

1 Put the sentences in order. Write 1–6.

a) Nigel flies away with Jewel. 5
b) Blu and Jewel dance. 3
c) Jewel bites Marcel. 2
d) Blu flies. 6
e) Blu goes to Rio. 1
f) Luiz helps Blu and Jewel. 4

2 Who says this? Write M for Marcel or N for Nigel.

a) 'Not one, but TWO blue Spix's Macaws!' M
b) 'Ow!' M
c) 'Horrible birds!' M
d) 'I've got you now!' N
e) 'Let's fly!' M
f) 'Stop!' N

Where's the popcorn?
Look in your book.
Can you find it? Yes, Page 26.

Puzzle time!

1 How many words can you make? Use the letters to make eight words from pages 4 and 5. You can use letters more than once.

bite	cage
fall	fly
free	kite
help	chain

2 Who does Blu meet first in the story? Put the characters in order.

2 

3 

4 

1 

5 

3 What is the bird doing? Match the words and the pictures.

a) He's eating.

b) He's dancing.

c) He's laughing.

d) He's flying.

e) He's falling.

i) 

ii) 

iii) 

iv) 

v) 

4a Who's this? Finish the picture.

b Do you like this character? Why / Why not?

Yes, cause she is beautiful and nice.

Imagine ...

1 Read the scene. Where are Blu and Jewel?

Blu	What are you doing?
Jewel	I want to be free!
Blu	No problem! I have a cage at home. I can do it!
Jewel	We're free!
Blu	No! I can't fly!
Jewel	Oh no!

2 Work with a friend. Act out the scene.

Chant

1 Listen and read.

Come to Rio!

Wow! It's Rio!
Rio is hot.
Come to Rio!
I like it a lot.

Wow ! It's Rio!
Fly away!
Come to Rio
With me today!

2 Say the chant.